Magic Ballerina

Holly and...

Welcome to the world of Enchantia!

I have always loved to dance. The captivating
music and wonderful stories of ballet are so
inspiring. So come with me and let's follow
Holly on her magical adventures in
Enchantia, where the stories of dance will
take you on a very special journey.

p.s. Turn to the back to learn a special
dance step from me...

Special thanks to
Ann Bryant and
Katie May

First published in Great Britain by HarperCollins *Children's Books* 2009
HarperCollins *Children's Books* is a division of HarperCollins *Publishers* Ltd,
1 London Bridge Street, London SE1 9GF

The HarperCollins website address is
www.harpercollins.co.uk

21

Text copyright © HarperCollins *Children's Books* 2009
Illustrations by Katie May
Illustrations copyright © HarperCollins *Children's Books* 2009

MAGIC BALLERINA™ and the 'Magic Ballerina' logo are
trademarks of HarperCollins Publishers Ltd.

ISBN-13 978 0 00 732323 4

Printed and bound by CPI Group (UK) Ltd, Croydon, CR0 4YY

Magic Ballerina

Holly and the Ice Palace

Darcey Bussell

HarperCollins *Children's Books*

*To Phoebe and Zoe, as they are the inspiration
behind Magic Ballerina.*

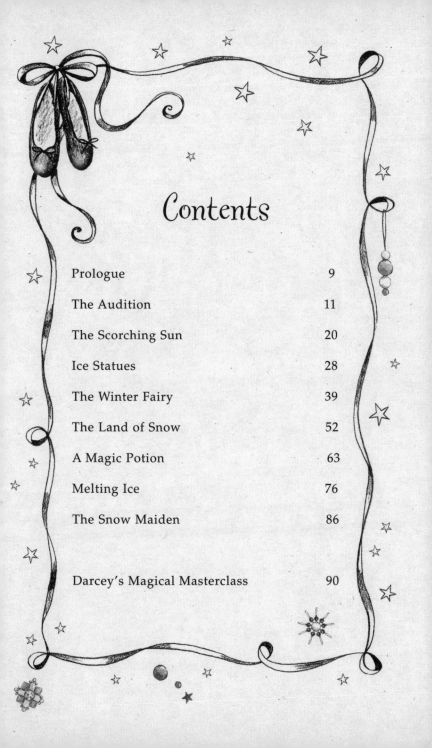

Contents

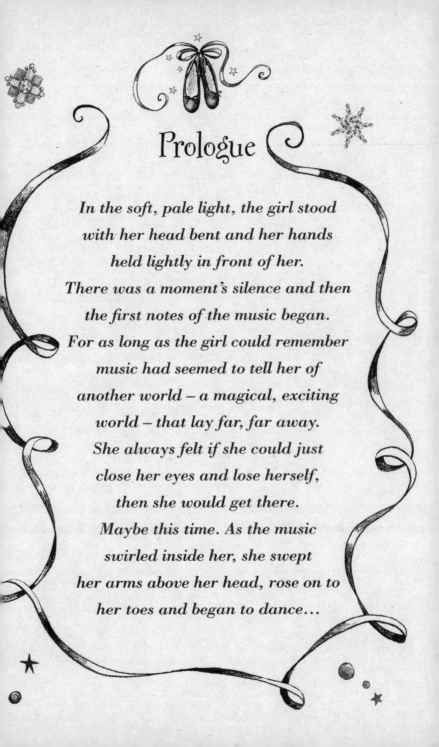

Prologue

In the soft, pale light, the girl stood
with her head bent and her hands
held lightly in front of her.
There was a moment's silence and then
the first notes of the music began.
For as long as the girl could remember
music had seemed to tell her of
another world – a magical, exciting
world – that lay far, far away.
She always felt if she could just
close her eyes and lose herself,
then she would get there.
Maybe this time. As the music
swirled inside her, she swept
her arms above her head, rose on to
her toes and began to dance…

The Audition

Holly Wilde ran excitedly up the steps of her ballet school. She was about to audition for the local production of *The Nutcracker*, which Madame Za-Za, her ballet teacher, was helping to produce, and there was one particular part that Holly was desperate to get. She could still feel the tight good-luck hug that her aunt

had given her at home a few moments
before.

"Just remember what your mum told
you," her aunt had said.

"Don't worry, I will!" Holly had replied,
nodding hard.

Holly's parents were both professional
ballet dancers. They had divorced and were
so often away on tour with their different
ballet companies that it was easier for Holly
to live with her aunt and uncle during term
time. Holly really missed her mum, but
whenever she felt sad she reminded herself
that they had two big things connecting
them. Firstly, they both loved each other,
and secondly, they totally loved ballet.

And I've got a special ballet secret all of my

own! thought Holly, as she pushed open the door to Madame Za-Za's. She glanced down at the red ballet shoes poking out of her bag and smiled. Her shoes had special powers – when they glowed it meant they were about to take Holly on a magical  journey to the Land of Enchantia, where all the characters from the ballets lived. It had happened quite a few times already, and each time Holly had an amazing adventure.

"Hi, Holly! Are you nervous? *I* am!" Her friend Chloe had caught up with her and they went into the changing rooms together.

"I do feel a bit nervous," admitted Holly. "But excited too. I've been practising like mad and I'm determined to get the part of a Snow Maiden."

"Me too," said Chloe, "but, you know, apart from us, it's only older students auditioning to be Snow Maidens."

Holly stared out of the window, suddenly wrapped up in a memory of the first time she'd ever seen *The Nutcracker*. Her mum had taken her to the theatre when she was only five, and she could still remember the magic thrill inside her at the sight of the Prince and Clara, travelling through the Land of Snow in a glittering magic sleigh on their way to the Land of Sweets.

But the Snow Maidens were even more magical than Clara and the Prince. They had seemed to float around the stage like the softest snowflakes as they'd danced.

Holly sighed at the lovely memory as she broke out of her daydream, then began to put on her silver-white tutu over her pale tights.

"Mum said the Waltz of the Snowflakes is very difficult," Holly told her friend. "She said it's important to listen to the music really carefully."

Chloe nodded, and the two girls warmed up until they were called into the studio.

"This is it!" whispered Chloe, going in first.

"Good luck!" mouthed Holly.

Then she gasped as she followed Chloe through the door. It was as though the studio had been transformed into the Land of Snow, with glistening scenery. Across one wall was a backdrop of icy silver and blue, covered with bright white snowflakes like stars.

In a flash, Holly felt herself transported
back to the theatre where she'd seen *The
Nutcracker* all those years ago.

I'm going to make you proud, Mum, she
said to herself, lifting her chin and feeling
determination rush through her as she
walked to her place.

"How do you think it went?" asked Chloe, clutching Holly's hand outside in the corridor when the audition was over.

Almost immediately, they were surrounded by other students. "What was it like? Did it go well?" they wanted to know.

Holly was going back over the audition in her head. She thought it had been all right, but you could never be sure.

"I took your mum's advice and focused on the music like mad," said Chloe, as she set off back to the changing rooms with the others.

Holly stopped in her tracks. It was as though she was glued to the spot. She'd just realised something awful. She'd been concentrating so hard on the steps and the expression, and feeling the icy atmosphere, that she hadn't even noticed the music. How could she have forgotten such an important thing? Especially when her mum had particularly drawn attention to it. She dropped her head sadly at her stupid mistake and immediately got another shock.

Her red shoes were glowing! That could only mean one thing – she was about to go to Enchantia. Right now!

The Scorching Sun

The glow was turning to swirls of colours, getting faster and brighter, and suddenly, Holly was swept up amongst them.

Where am I? she thought, a few moments later.

The field where she had landed was completely deserted. There weren't even any trees in it, which was a shame, because the sun was beating down furiously and Holly was dying for a bit of shade. Her friend the White Cat was nowhere to be seen either, but he'd arrive at any moment, she was sure. He usually did.

I hope he gets here soon, thought Holly, as the heat started to make her feel a bit faint. Thank goodness she was still in her Snow Maiden outfit or she'd boil over. Even the grass was wilting and beginning to turn brown.

Just when Holly thought she'd melt if she didn't find some shade, a familiar voice sounded just behind her.

"Hello! Hello!"

The White Cat was leaping towards her. Holly could tell he was happy to see her, but it was also clear he was anxious about something.

"Oh, Cat!" she said, shaking his paw gently. "Sorry, too hot for hugs! Whatever's going on?"

"Big problem!" said the White Cat, fanning himself with his tail. "Terrible magic afoot."

Holly knew that the shoes only brought her to Enchantia if there was something the matter, and wondered what on earth could be making her friend sound so worked up.

"You see that palace up on the hill over there?" he went on, a bit breathlessly.

Holly followed his gaze. She could just make out the most enormous building surrounded by snow clouds, far in the distance.

"That is the home of King Rat," explained the White Cat.

Holly turned sharply at the sound of the name. She had heard of an evil King Rat from *The Nutcracker*. "He set his army of mice on to the Nutcracker Prince, didn't he?" she said.

The White Cat nodded. "Those mouse guards of his are very fierce, with sabre swords and lashing tails. And King Rat himself is really disliked here in Enchantia. He doesn't like dancing, you see, so he's forever spoiling things for us."

Holly's eyes widened as she looked back at the hill in the distance. "And that's where he lives?"

"Well," said the White Cat. "He actually lived in a grey stone castle until recently. But he is so vain and selfish, and absolutely

has to have whatever he wants. So his latest evil trick has been to capture the magic powers of the Winter Fairy from *Cinderella* and use them to transform his castle into an Ice Palace!"

Holly was shocked. "I've met the Winter Fairy," she said. "And the Summer Fairy too. They were at the christening of Cinderella's little baby, Pearl, weren't they?"

"That's right," said the White Cat, nodding. Then his anxious look returned. "The trouble is," he went on, wiping his forehead with his paw, "it is the joint powers of the Winter Fairy and the Summer Fairy that control the temperature and the seasons in Enchantia. Now that the Winter

Fairy's powers have been snatched away,
the Summer Fairy's powers have taken
over. The whole land can hardly breathe,
it's so hot. The two sets of powers balance
each other out, you see. That's just the way
it works."

Holly had been trying to take in all that
the White Cat was saying, but it wasn't
easy when she felt as though she was about
to faint from the heat.

"We have to get the Winter Fairy's
powers back," she said, trying to sound
stronger than she felt. "We must go to the
Ice Palace immediately!"

Her friend nodded. "You're absolutely
right!"

But his anxious expression quickly

returned. "We mustn't get too close, though. You've no idea how strong King Rat's powers are, especially in his own territory. I'll magic us to somewhere nearby, just to be safe."

Holly nodded and watched, as her friend drew a circle with his tail, swishing it through the long dry grass. Then she stepped inside the circle. The last thing she saw of the field was a cloud of golden sparks that whirled in a haze, lighting the tips of the blades of grass.

Ice Statues

"This is as close as I dare to get," said the White Cat.

Holly didn't answer. She was too busy staring in awe at the magnificent ice palace in front of them. Its turrets and towers glowed and gleamed in silver brilliance, and, through the tall ice-spiked gates, she could see a winter garden full of ice sculptures.

"They're not real sculptures," the White Cat whispered, following Holly's gaze. "They're people that King Rat has turned into statues with his evil magic."

Holly gasped. Anger flared up inside her at this nasty cruel rat, but she was puzzled too. "What were these people doing here in the first place?" she asked.

"They each came to try and rescue the Winter Fairy," said the White Cat. "Everyone is so alarmed about how Enchantia is heating up that they're desperate to restore the natural balance of the seasons. But see what's become of them!"

"No, look, they're not all ice statues!" said Holly, suddenly spotting a young man who had appeared from round the side of the garden. He was looking furtively this way and that, as he dodged behind one ice statue after another.

"He'll be searching for the Winter Fairy," said the White Cat, in a low voice. "Just like the others."

"Oh, dear, I hope he manages to keep himself hidden, so he doesn't get turned into a—"

But Holly never had a chance to finish her sentence. Instead, she gasped because the man was halfway between two statues

when the front door of the palace was
suddenly flung open, and there stood
King Rat himself. His beady red eyes
stared out from beneath grey bushy
eyebrows. Whiskers sprouted from all
over his face. And on his head perched a
tall golden crown, which Holly thought
looked ridiculous.

Spotting the intruder, his face turned
purple with anger and he began yelling a
chant as he swiped his sword through the
air.

"Once I swish again and twice.
Now turn this mad fool into ice!"
In a flash, the man became a statue,
and Holly shivered at the terrible
sight.

"He still looks real!" she said through chattering teeth as she drew closer to her friend.

The White Cat nodded grimly. "You see

what I mean about King Rat's powers," he
whispered.

Holly shivered again, which made her
"Yes!" come out louder than
she'd intended. Her hand
flew to her mouth as
King Rat turned sharply,
scanning the grounds with
his beady eyes.

"Don't let him see you!" hissed the White
Cat, pulling Holly down behind one of the
ice fir trees at the gate. And there they
crouched, listening to King Rat's angry
voice, coming from much closer to them
now.

"I tell you, you're useless! No good to me
at all!"

Holly wondered for a moment if King Rat was talking to *her*, but she knew he couldn't possibly be, and strained her ears for the sound of a reply. But there wasn't one.

"You're supposed to have all this special power, so use it, you dim-witted drip!"

Again there was no reply.

"How can it have run out? Answer me!" he went on, his tone getting crosser with every word he uttered.

"Who's he shouting at?" Holly whispered tremulously.

Keeping very low, the two of them cautiously popped their heads around the side of the tree. There was only King Rat to be seen, however, and he wasn't looking in their direction. It was a struggle for Holly not to giggle now she could properly see his outfit. He was wearing a tight, sequined skating suit of vivid red and gold, and tottering about on a pair of ice skates. She cupped her hand over her mouth and spoke into the White Cat's ear, trying not to splutter. "Maybe he's talking to himself! Doesn't he look silly!"

"Oh, no!" There was something in the urgent tone of Cat's voice that silenced Holly in a second. And when she saw for herself what had caught his eye, her hand shot to her mouth.

The Winter Fairy had come into view. She was leaning against one of the ice statues, her wings drooping, her wand hanging limply at her side, while King Rat carried on.

"You utterly feeble faded fairy! What kind of a creature are you?" He stamped his foot and thrust his sharp ugly nose almost into the poor fairy's face, then stomped off clumsily on his skates towards the frozen moat.

Holly couldn't understand what he was so furious about. Then, right before her eyes, the Winter Fairy slid to the ground at the foot of the ice statue, in a total faint.

The Winter Fairy

"Oh, my glittering whiskers!" said the White Cat. "We must go to her!"

Holly didn't need telling twice. The two of them jumped out from behind the fir tree, but immediately stopped in their tracks at the sound of a great bellow from the direction of the moat.

"Guards! I fancy a ride! I need you to

pull my sleigh! Come on! Get a move on!"

Eight mouse guards instantly came running out of the palace and raced off towards the moat, to attend to their bossy king. The moment they were out of sight, Holly and the White Cat rushed to the fairy's side and bent down. Her frightened eyes fluttered open, then closed gently.

"Don't worry," whispered the White Cat, gathering her up.

"Let me help," said Holly.

"It's all right, she's light as a feather," the White Cat answered. "Just keep your eye on the moat. We mustn't be seen."

A minute later, they were safely back a little distance outside the grounds of the ice palace, the Winter Fairy sitting with her

head in her hand, crying softly.

"Oh, whatever is to become of Enchantia?" she managed between sobs.

The White Cat patted her hand with his paw. "There, there!" he said. "Let's worry about that later. First things first. We want you to get better." And with a swish of his

tail, he magicked up a delicious

meal of sweet berries

and honey with a

glass of rosewater to

accompany it.

The fairy drank and ate very slowly, and after a few moments, close to tears again, she sighed and murmured, "It's no good. I don't have the energy to eat any more."

"Oh, dear, how can we help?" Holly asked anxiously.

"You remember Holly, don't you?" the White Cat said gently to the fairy. "She's the human owner of the magic ballet shoes."

The fairy gave a tiny nod and managed the smallest of smiles, then began to talk in such a thin voice that Holly and the White

Cat had to lean forward to hear what she was saying.

"King Rat sapped me of my winter powers to create his ice palace," she said. "Only now, he's furious that all my power has run out and he can't get the other ice things he wants."

"But it's *you* we're worried about," said Holly, touching the fairy's frail hand. "We want you and Enchantia to be restored to normal. Never mind King Rat and his stupid demands."

"Quite right," agreed the White Cat, his eyes glinting.

The fairy's eyelashes fluttered again. "There's only one way that my powers can be restored, and the rest of Enchantia can be prevented from heating up until it's too hot to bear," she said in her tiny cracked voice.

Holly and the White Cat bent closer, eager to hear.

The fairy drew a shallow breath. "I must drink from the secret Winter Power potion that is hidden deep in the heart of the Land of Snow…"

Holly felt a mixture of respect and sorrow for the fairy. There she was, fading away before their eyes, and yet she was still only concerned about helping Enchantia.

"Try a little more food," Holly urged. "Then perhaps you can take us there."

The fairy blinked once or twice, as though she was trying to wake herself up. "I'm sorry," she said, shaking her head sadly. "I am just too weak to travel."

"Well, if you could tell us where to find the secret remedy, we could go ourselves," Holly cried.

"It's… in a… lantern…" The fairy's words were fainter than ever.

"Yes, a lantern. Where exactly?" said Holly.

"Impossible to explain…" came the

answer in the tiniest thread of a voice.

"Is there nothing you can tell us to help us find it?" asked the White Cat gently, as Holly swallowed, feeling a great fear mounting inside her. She knew that it was her job to help sort out the problem whenever she was called to Enchantia. She had always managed before, but this time it was looking as though she might fail. And that was unthinkable.

The fairy was trying to say something, but it was impossible to hear, so Holly put her ear right to her mouth.

"Listen…" whispered the fairy.

"Yes, I'm listening," said Holly, waiting to hear more.

But the fairy just closed her eyes and

Holly exchanged a fearful look with the White Cat.

"Right," he announced, suddenly jumping up. "We will be back in two shakes of a lamb's tail."

Holly knew he was only sounding brave so the fairy wouldn't worry even more. However were they going to manage to find a lantern in the Land of Snow?

And now there seemed to be another problem. The White Cat was drawing a circle in the frost outside the palace gates with his tail. His whiskers were twitching and his eyes glittering. Holly knew he would be conjuring up a picture of the Land of Snow, so he could magic them both there. So why was nothing happening? She threw him a questioning look.

"It doesn't seem to be working," he murmured, flicking his tail impatiently against the ground.

After watching him try again without success, Holly suddenly remembered something from *The Nutcracker*. "Do you think we need to travel in a sleigh?" she offered uncertainly. "That's the way Clara and the Prince get to the Land of Snow."

"Yes! Yes! Of course! You're absolutely right!" said the White Cat, clapping his paws together and jumping into the air, crossing his feet over and over. As he landed, a magnificent sparkling sleigh of white and gold appeared before them and they both climbed on.

"Silly me. Should have thought of that!" he muttered as he took his place. "There's only one way to get to the Land of Snow and that's in a sleigh. Normal magic won't work."

"We'll be back as quickly as we can be!"
said Holly to the fairy, who opened her
eyes for just a second to give them a grateful
smile.

Then away they went, up into the sky,
until they were looking down on the
glittering Ice Palace and the statues.

As they flew a little higher, the moat on
the far side of the palace came into view.
Holly's eyes widened at the sight of the

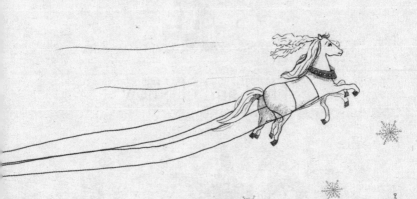

struggling, straining figures of the mouse guards. They were attached to an enormous sleigh and were dragging it along. King Rat lay on his back in the centre of the sleigh, ankles crossed, hands behind his head. His nasty rodent nose was pointed up to the sky, and Holly gasped with shock as she realised the rat's sharp, beady eyes were staring straight at her. She ducked down, but it was too late. He had definitely seen her!

The Land of Snow

"He saw us! King Rat saw us!" Holly uttered shakily. "What if he follows us?"

"He doesn't know where we're going, remember," the White Cat reassured Holly. "And even if he got curious and decided to find out, he'd never be able to catch up. We're way ahead. Anyway, you can't see a thing in this snow!"

It was true, now they were entering the
Land of Snow, there were thick snowflakes
swirling all around them and they could
hardly see further than their noses.

Holly's heart began to beat a little faster.
"Do you… know where we are, Cat?" she
asked.

"Yes, we're flying over the forest. Look!"
he replied. He was sitting up straight and
seemed perfectly in control to Holly.

The sleigh brushed the feathery tops of
the tall fir trees as it zoomed along. But as
the snowflakes began to swirl more and
more wildly, Holly glanced at the White Cat
again, to check he still looked confident.
*How on earth will we ever find the potion in
this blizzard?* she thought to herself.

When the White Cat's eyes started to flick anxiously from side to side, Holly's heart sank.

"Are we lost?" she asked.

The White Cat didn't reply, but she noticed that his whiskers were twitching just the tiniest bit, which usually meant that magic was afoot. And a moment later, Holly realised that something had changed. She sat up straighter and looked around her in amazement, a rush of wonder and delight swelling up inside her. The swirling snowflakes no longer swirled. In fact, they weren't snowflakes at all. They had become dancing maidens, floating around as light as the air.

Holly caught her breath. They were the Snow Maidens!

"Can you show us the way to the centre of your land, please?" she called out to the Snow Maidens who were gracefully pirouetting in the frosty air, hearing the urgency in her own voice. She'd suddenly remembered the poor Winter Fairy fading away, all alone in the icy outskirts of King Rat's domain.

There was no reply from the Snow Maidens, and the White Cat whispered out of the corner of his mouth that they couldn't speak. Holly felt her mind cast right back to the time she'd watched the dancers in the theatre with her mum. And now, here she was, flying amongst the real Snow Maidens as they bobbed and flitted and floated in graceful curtsies and soft whirls. And as she watched them, she suddenly realised that there was music in the air. It was faint and distant-sounding, but it was definitely there.

"Did you hear that, Cat?" she breathed.

The White Cat cocked his head, his ears

twitching, then frowned. "Hear what? I
don't hear a thing!"

"Music!" said Holly, concentrating hard
with every bone in her body. And that was
when she noticed something wonderful.
The Snow Maidens were rising and falling
in time to the music.

Holly's heart beat faster as a feeling of
understanding came to her. "Can you hold
the sleigh still, Cat?" she asked him. "I need
to follow their dance."

The White Cat looked puzzled, but nodded in agreement. Holly carefully stood up, concentrated on the rhythm and tried to relax and let herself go with the flow of the music. It felt magic, especially when Holly realised something else as she danced. The Snow Maidens were smiling and unfurling their arms slowly and gracefully, as though pointing the way. Listening with all her might Holly continued to dance, and, following the direction of their outstretched arms,

the White Cat steered the sleigh to the very heart of the Land of Snow. A moment later, the sleigh began to float gently down amongst the trees.

The music has stopped, thought Holly, tuning into the breathless hush.

Then, "Look! There it is!" came the voice of the White Cat, a little muffled in the dense white world.

Holly followed his gaze. Hanging from a slender branch, almost hidden from view, was a white lantern, which cast a soft yellow glow upon the thick snow.

"We've found it!" breathed Holly. "We've actually found it!"

As the sleigh hovered above the pool of light, Holly carefully opened the door of

the lantern and took out the tiny bottle of
potion that nestled inside. She and the
White Cat grinned at each other.

"Well done!" he said, excitement in his
voice.

"Now just the return journey to make,"
said Holly.

"Yes, and now it's my turn to do a bit of
work!" said the White Cat. "I'm sure I can

find the way back to the Winter Fairy. You have a rest. You certainly deserve it!"

Holly lay back gratefully against the comfy padded seat in the sleigh. "It's true, I was concentrating so hard on listening to the music when I danced, I'm exhausted," she said. Then she sat bolt upright again as something hit her. "Of course, that's it!" she cried. "That's what the Winter Fairy meant when she said, 'Listen…' I thought she meant *listen to the important thing I'm about to tell you*. But that *was* the important thing. I had to *listen to the music!*" Holly smiled to herself.

But the smile waned at the sight of another sleigh, an enormous one, zooming towards them. Then her stomach turned over as the features of the driver came into view. A dark brown pointy face. Nasty, piggy eyes.

King Rat.

A Magic Potion

"Oh, my shimmering whiskers! Look who he's got in the sleigh with him!" said the White Cat, a note of alarm in his voice.

Holly gasped. Beside the repulsive Rat, looking pale and weak, sat the Winter Fairy.

"Now what do we do, Cat?" Holly felt herself tense up and her next words came out in a loud, urgent voice. "We have to get the magic potion to the Winter Fairy! We absolutely have to!" Then she faltered a little. "Only how can we approach her when she's with King Rat? And what's he doing here, anyway?"

"He must have forced the Winter Fairy to tell him what you and I were up to when he spied us leaving his Ice Palace in our sleigh," said the White Cat, his mouth set in a thin line.

Holly nodded fearfully. "And now he's after us, trying to grab the potion and stop our mission." She spoke more quickly. "We've got to get away from him…" Then her eyes flickered uncertainly, "… and yet we've got to get to the fairy. But it's impossible to do both, because they're side

by side in that enormous sleigh that's
getting closer and closer to us by the
second! Oh, Cat, whatever we do, we can't
win!"

The two of them watched, their hearts in
their mouths, as the grand and glittering
sleigh came swooping down upon them.
And in that second, Holly knew she had to

think of something immediately.

"Keep him talking," she told the White Cat urgently, "while I try to smuggle the magic potion to the Winter Fairy."

"Good afternoon, Your Majesty!" the White Cat called cheerily, bowing his head respectfully.

Holly couldn't help noticing how King Rat instantly puffed up. He obviously liked to be recognised and respected.

"I do hope you're enjoying showing your… er… friend around the Land of Snow, as much as my friend and I are enjoying it, Your Majesty!" went on the White Cat, in his politest tone.

The sleighs drew level with each other.

"Huh! I wouldn't enjoy it in *that* ridiculously little sleigh!" the vain King Rat replied.

"Well, yes, yours is certainly much the grander of the two!" agreed the White Cat, as Holly subtly signalled to the fairy that she had the potion. The fairy's eyes widened and Holly could see she understood, but how was she going to get the potion to her?

King Rat was still distracted, boasting about his sleigh. "Not only is it grander, it is faster and it has more gold on it too."

Holly had never thought so quickly in all her life. "It is, but what's that rushing noise?" she cried. "It sounds just like the noise our sleigh made earlier on when we nearly crashed, doesn't it, Cat?"

She gave the White Cat a meaningful look and, to her relief, he seemed to understand. "Absolutely the same sound!" he agreed, nodding hard. "But it's definitely not *our* sleigh. No, no, ours is fine now we've lightened it."

"Then it must be *your* sleigh, Your

Majesty!" said Holly. "Oh, dear! I'm so sorry!"

"Mine? Mine? What are you talking about?" King Rat cried, rocking the sleigh violently as he threw himself from one side to the other, trying to look over the edge.

"It's all right, you just need to lighten the sleigh by throwing something out," went on Holly smoothly. "That will cure the problem."

"Yes, we threw out a blanket, and that certainly did the trick!" said the White Cat cheerily. "Do you have anything you can throw out, Your Majesty?" he added innocently, whilst twitching his sparkling whiskers.

King Rat's eyes darted this way and that, until finally they settled on the fairy. Holly didn't dare look across at the White Cat as he performed his magic. Was their plan going to work?

Finally, King Rat spoke. "You'll have to get out…" he said to the Winter Fairy. "Just until this problem with the sleigh is sorted."

Holly could hardly contain herself. But then she saw the look in the poor fairy's eyes. It was a mixture of fear that she wouldn't have the strength to fly, and something else that Holly couldn't fathom. But a moment later, the fairy spread her wings and seemed to float out of King Rat's sleigh.

"Well, I can't imagine that making any difference!" King Rat muttered, as he kept rocking from side to side, in his clumsy attempts to see what was happening to his sleigh.

While he was distracted, the White Cat took the chance to lower their sleigh until it was in the perfect position for the fairy to float straight into. Holly watched her glide weakly down through the snowflakes, and come to rest right beside her, with her wings folded, her head lowered wearily.

"Drink this!" Holly whispered urgently, handing the magic potion to the fairy. "Hurry!"

The moment the Winter Fairy had swallowed the potion, the White Cat cried out, "Right, hold on tight!" And there was an enormous jolt that made Holly and the fairy clutch each other tight for a few seconds. Then they fell apart, wide-eyed at the sound of King Rat shouting his head off.

"What did you do to his sleigh, Cat?" asked Holly, as they zipped smoothly away through the white clouds.

"I thought he might enjoy a quick spin!" answered the laughing White Cat, as all three of them turned to see the Rat's enormous sleigh whizzing round and round like a crazy merry-go-round.

The fairy smiled a bright smile and Holly

couldn't believe how quickly she'd changed. In no time at all, the potion had clearly done its work. She was no longer a fragile fading thing, but a twinkling feisty fairy, beginning to flutter and light up with life.

"Oh, you're better!" cried Holly happily. "Enchantia will be restored to normal now!"

But the fairy didn't have a chance to say anything in reply. Suddenly, they all froze with fear at the sound of King Rat's furious voice, frighteningly close to them.

"You wait, you three! I'm coming to get you! Right now!"

Holly turned to see that the enormous

great sleigh had stopped spinning and was
zooming towards them, cutting through the
air like a massive torpedo.

Melting Ice

"Oh, no!" said Holly.

"Oh, my glimmering tail!" squeaked the White Cat.

"Hold my hands!" commanded the fairy.

Holly and the White Cat immediately did as they were told.

"Oh, my…"

There was a flash and a whoosh and the

next thing they knew, all three of them were standing in the very field that Holly had first found herself in, when she'd arrived in Enchantia. Only now the grass was lush and green, and the sun was shining pleasantly, warming them with a soft gentle heat.

"Oh, my beating heart!" said the White Cat a little shakily.

"We're safe now," said the Winter Fairy, letting go of his paw.

Holly took a deep breath to calm herself. "How did you do that?" she asked, turning round slowly, but not letting go of the fairy's hand. She couldn't believe that she had come so speedily from cold Winter and terrible fear to warm Spring and safety.

"My powers are strongest in the Land of Snow," the fairy replied with a smile. "And once I'd drunk the magic potion and restored myself, there was nothing more King Rat could do to harm us. When you held my hands, my powers flowed through you too. I simply magicked us out of King Rat's clutches!"

Then she looked properly at Holly. "I don't know what I would have done without you," she said gratefully. "It was incredible the way you managed to find the magic potion."

Something was still troubling Holly, though. "What if he captures you again?" she asked anxiously.

The fairy smiled. "There is no more potion left. I hold the Power of Winter

inside me forever! There is nothing King
Rat or anyone can do to alter the balance in
Enchantia now. So, I thank you both from
the bottom of my heart."

Holly felt a surge of
something peaceful inside
her and smiled back at the
fairy. "Good, because I
don't like that mean old rat
and his nasty magic!" she said.

The fairy gave a tinkly laugh. "Well," she
said, "somehow, I don't think King Rat will
be in the mood for doing any magic – nasty
or otherwise – when he sees what has
happened back at his 'Ice Palace'!"

Holly wanted to know what the fairy
meant, so the White Cat drew a circle with

his tail on the bright green grass.
Immediately, a mist rose up inside the
magic ring, then it slowly began to clear,
revealing King Rat's Ice Palace. Holly
gasped as she watched the scene at the
palace unfold. The glistening ice was
melting and water was trickling down the
sides of the building. But it wasn't clear
sparkling water, it was grey and murky.

Before their eyes, the Ice Palace was vanishing and in its place, a grim grey old castle was taking shape.

"That's King Rat's *real* home!" said the White Cat.

Holly's eyes were wide. "I can hear angry shouting," she said, still peering into the circle at the incredible scene.

"Look, there! In the moat!" said the White Cat, pointing.

And Holly laughed at the sight of a sunken sleigh and King Rat flailing about, splashing the water and yelling, "Get me out of here, you buffoons!"

His mouse guards were trying their best to help him out of the water, but his wild kicks were soaking them.

All the ice statues had melted and the people trapped inside them were cheerfully heading home.

Then the scene began to fade and the distant yells of King Rat became fainter. "Where has my palace gone? Why is everything melting?" His words seemed to fly like sharp pins off the cold stone walls of his castle.

"I think we've seen enough," laughed the White Cat, "don't you?" And with that, he gathered up his tail and gave it a quick twirl before leaping into the air. Holly watched his legs criss-cross at least six times at the ankles. By the time he landed in a perfect *demi-plié*, the scene before them had completely disappeared.

The fairy sighed happily. "We shall have a party in your honour, Holly, to thank you for helping to restore the balance in our land. In fact, I can hear the music beginning already!"

Holly listened. Yes, there was definitely music in the air. But something else was happening too. Her feet had started to tingle and she knew that this was one party she would have to miss.

"It's time for me to go back," she said quietly. "But I'll think of you and imagine you all dancing…"

"… while King Rat sulks in his horrid old castle!" added the White Cat, chuckling to himself.

"Yes," laughed Holly. "And I'll be back soon, I'm sure."

Her dear friend hugged her and the fairy placed a fluttery kiss on her cheek. Then Holly rose up in a mass of sparkles, the music still sounding in her ears, a soft lilting melody, as light and floaty as a snowflake.

The Snow Maiden

A second later, Holly found herself right
back in the corridor outside the studio
where she'd just done the audition. As
always, when she returned from Enchantia,
no time at all had passed in the real world.
She felt as though she could still hear the
tinkling snow music, though.

But a second later it faded and in its

Holly and the Ice Palace

place came the sound of her teacher's voice.
"Ah, there you are, Holly! I just wanted to
tell you and Chloe that I've decided you
both auditioned well enough to take the
roles of Snow Maidens, along with the
older girls in the production. Your dancing
was beautifully expressive and, as you
learn to listen to the music more, you will
be perfect."

Holly felt a lovely thrill go zapping
through her. "Oh, thank you, Madame Za-Za!
Thank you so much. I promise I'll listen as
hard as I possibly can from now on!"

And she smiled to herself, quite certain
that she truly knew how important it was
to listen to the music. She would never ever
forget her time with the Snow Maidens in

Enchantia. They would inspire her to dance their dance with all her heart. And the best thing of all was that her mum would be back in time for the show. She couldn't wait!

Tiptoe over the page to learn

a special dance step...

Darcey's Magical Masterclass

Grands Battements Derriére

Try to create a beautiful shape with your leg, sweeping it up and then down in this graceful step, always keeping your knees straight.

1.
Start in first position, facing the barre and holding on lightly with both hands for balance.

2.
Keeping tall, extend your right leg out behind you, as high off the ground as you can. Point your toes and your upper body will naturally tip forwards.

3.
Then lower your leg and your body will straighten back up again. Come to rest with your feet in first position.

4.
Repeat this step three times and then change legs.

Everything's gone topsy-turvy in the Land
of Sweets! Can Holly and her friend put
things right before the carnival begins?

**Read on for a sneak preview
of Holly's next adventure...**

Holly turned right round and gasped, because a gigantic palace that looked like it was made of white icing stood gleaming and tall against the bright blue sky. Holly pinched herself to check she wasn't dreaming. But she really was in Enchantia, because there was her friend, the White Cat, standing beside her.

"Oh Cat, where are we?" She looked round in awe. "This is incredible!"

The White Cat chuckled and looked proud. "The Land of Sweets!" he told her.

As Holly looked around her, she realised she could probably have worked that out for herself. There were mountains topped with whipped cream, flowers glazed with frosted syrup, fountains of sherbet, lollipop trees, candy-cane sticks of rock, jelly houses, fields of golden popcorn, even valleys of marshmallows.

"Oh, Cat! It's deliciously... amazing!"

"Not at the moment, it isn't," said the White Cat, looking downcast. "Come with me."

Holly was puzzled. She followed him down a sweeping drive of pink and white coconut flakes, into the palace. The grand reception hall was decorated with piped icing, and Holly couldn't believe the magnificent ballroom that the White Cat was leading her into. Enormous pillars studded with multi-coloured fruit pastilles reached up to a caramel-coated ceiling. The floor was made of hard shiny toffee, the walls, of Turkish delight.

But when Holly managed to drag her eyes away from all the splendour, she saw that something was going wrong here. In the middle of the room were groups of dancing Sweets, desperately trying to stay on their feet, but failing. White Chocolate Whirlers were dancing to Spanish music with clicking castanets, but they kept losing their balance and whirling off. Coffee dancers, dressed in wide silky trousers with little beaded tops and long flowing veils, were dancing to exotic Arabian music. Their veils had got all tangled up, though, and there was nothing graceful about the way they tried to pull apart from one another.

Holly turned in horror to the White Cat and gasped. "Whatever is going on?"

Magic Ballerina ™

Read all of Holly's adventures!